Mr. Waldorf is a lovable and inquisitive canine on a voyage to see not only the United States, but also International worlds of wonder. On this adventure, Mr. Waldorf discovers the mysterious China. The curious canine encounters fun new friends and places while visiting Beijing, discovering the Great Wall of China, climbing Mount Everest and traveling the Yangtze River.

Silly Mr. Waldorf has a tendency to misplace his favorite reading spectacles and can't seem to find them while discovering "The Peoples Republic of China". Mr. Waldorf will learn all about China, while seeking his missing spectacles. Will you help him find them and learn all about the ancient and beautiful country?

Children will fall in love with curious Mr. Waldorf and they will also discover the world in a fun and exciting way. Mr. Waldorf invites you to join his "Whoofishly" fun adventures! Where will the curious canine end up next?

Published by Waldorf Publishing

2140 Hall Johnson Road
#102-345
Grapevine, Texas 76051
www.WaldorfPublishing.com

The Spectacular World of Waldorf:
Mr. Waldorf Travels to the Mysterious China

ISBN: 9781943277636

Library of Congress Control Number: 2015957018

Copyright © 2016

The Spectacular World of Waldorf

Mr. Waldorf Travels to the Mysterious China

by

Beth Ann Stifflemire

&

Barbara Terry

Mr. Waldorf waves goodbye to Mr. River Pig and continues on his way toward the great mountain peak.

Mr. Waldorf has made it.
He's climbed Mount Everest.
"I did it!" Mr. Waldorf exclaims.
He looks all around him at
the amazing site below.
But still he has not found
his missing spectacles.

Author Bios

Beth Ann Stifflemire is a published fiction author ranging from Romance to Children's genres. A Communications Graduate of Texas A&M University, Beth Ann has been featured in the Austin American Statesman, Monster.com, Texas Wine Trail, Texas A&M University Communications Department Feature, Georgetown View Magazine, Hill Country News, Lone Star Literary Life and Nerd Girl Books and more. In addition she blogs at TheWritingTexan.com about everything from her writing journey to her favorite things in hopes it will inspire other Authors along the way.

Beth Ann changed the course of her life in 2010 after creating a Bucket List which included writing a book. It was merely the first step in uncovering her true calling and numerous titles and projects have developed from it. After over a decade involved in the corporate world, Beth Ann's spread her wings and tackled her true career as an Author.

Barbara Terry is one of the most sought-after Auto Experts, Columnists, Producers, Show Hosts, Authors and Off Road Racers. She has appeared on the cover of Kiplinger's Magazine, has been featured in over 100 publications and has made more than 1200 Television and Radio appearances since 2006 such as: Fox Sports, The CBS Early Show, Inside Edition, NBC, ABC, FOX, CBS, The Tony Danza Show, CNN, Maxim Radio, Oprah Radio, ESPN Radio, ivillage, SPEEDtv.com among a long list of others. She wrote a weekly auto advice column for The Houston Chronicle for 6 years, has written for Examiner.com, First30Days.com, motorolaroadtrips.com, Men's Fitness Magazine, New York Daily News and wrote a chapter in "The Experts Guide". Barbara owns and operates her own off road race team "Barbara Terry Racing" where her and her team participate in Off Road Races. She is the author of a hit book that hit book stores in August 2010 that features 40 Celebrity Athletes and their amazing car history, **"How Athletes Roll"**.

Barbara decided after a 10 year career in the Automotive Industry as a Professional Auto Expert, Spokesperson, Off Road Racer, Columnist, Producer, Show Host and Author that starting a Publishing Company was only fitting!